THE BEEZ BROTHERS

Copyright © 2022 by Celeste Johnson

ISBN: 978-1-998784-71-4 (Paperback)

All rights reserved. No part of this publication may be reproduced, distributed, or transmitted in any form or by any means, including photocopying, recording, or other electronic or mechanical methods, without the prior written permission of the publisher, except in the case brief quotations embodied in critical reviews and other noncommercial uses permitted by copyright law.

The views expressed in this book are solely those of the author and do not necessarily reflect the views of the publisher, and the publisher hereby disclaims any responsibility for them.

BookSide Press
877-741-8091
www.booksidepress.com
orders@booksidepress.com

Dedicated to my
Great-Grandchildren

My Beez Brothers:

Bryson

Braylin

Brandon

Brian

ROD-GI-BO PRODUCTIONS

Baby Brother Has AUTISM

WRITTEN AND ILLUSTRATED BY CELESTE

Mama Beez and the new baby came home from the hospital. The Beez brothers were so happy!

2-Bits, 4-Bits, and 6-Bits loved to make him smile.

But what he liked to do most was watch TV. He quietly sat and watched, never making any sounds.

When Dollar Bill went to Day Care he didn't play with the other children. The teacher tried to help him improve his social skills. She tried to get him interested in what the other children were doing. But he paid no attention to anything going on around him. He would look and then go back to what he was doing.

No matter how much fun the other children were having, Dollar Bill showed no interest.

Playing alone with his toys and watching TV were his favorite things to do.

2-Bits, 4-Bits, and 6-Bits got off the school bus. They hurried inside the Day Care to give Dollar Bill the treat they brought him.

Dollar Bill is always happy to see his brothers. He smiles at them and goes right back to watching TV.

Dollar Bill never tried to speak. He didn't make baby sounds that other babies made…such as Mama, Goo-goo or Da-Da. When he wanted something, he took you by the hand and led you to what he wanted.

At home, Dollar Bill didn't notice what his mother or brothers did…..He played with his toys and stayed quite. Mama Beez thought he was a very good baby because he never cried.

At 2 years old, Dollar Bill began to take toys or whatever he wanted from his brothers and other children.

He enjoyed playing with cars and shoes and putting them in a straight line, playing with his connector blocks was another of his favorite things to do.

Dollar Bill loved riding the bus. Dollar Bill only wanted to do things and go places that were familiar to him. Loud noises or anything new frightened him.

Dollar Bill enjoyed riding with 4-Bits on the scooter. He liked riding in cars, too.

Dollar Bill was two years old and still in diapers. Mama Beez tried very hard to potty train him.

Dollar Bill didn't like that at all! He cried whenever Mama Beez sat him on the potty.

Mama Beez told Daddy Beez how worried she was about Dollar Bill's slow development. At two years old, he wasn't talking; not potty trained, and his social skills were very bad. And the stimming….jumping and the noises he made.

Auntie Gina told her to take him to the doctor. She thought he might be autistic.

The doctor told Mama Beez that Dollar Bill was a healthy little boy but he was autistic. He wanted her to take him to a psychologist to be evaluated for autism.

He gave her a pamphlet to take home to read and to discuss it with the family because the entire family needed to understand an autistic child.

Dollar Bill had fun when the therapist started coming to the home. He liked to play with the toys the therapist used for training.

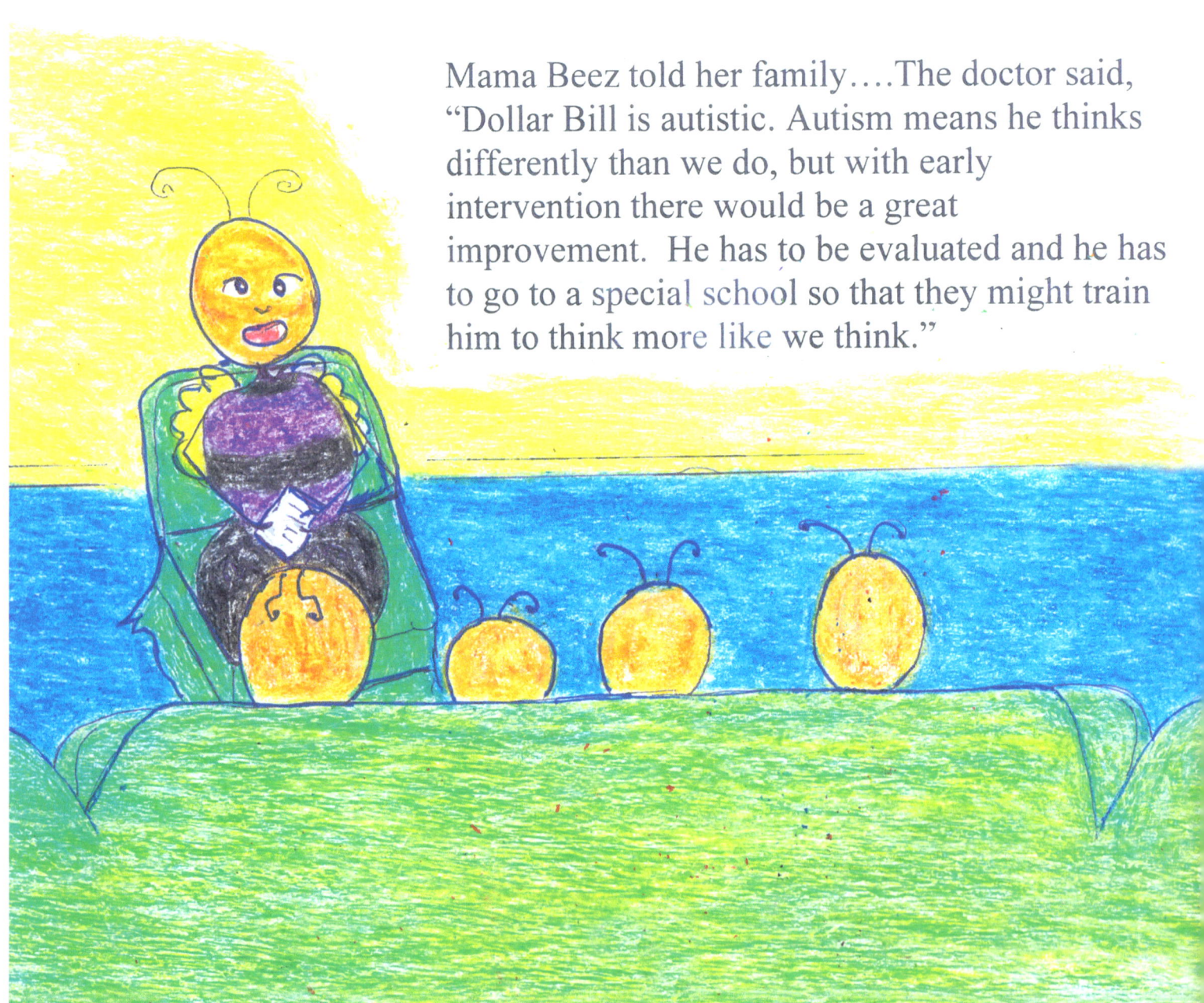

Mama Beez told her family….The doctor said, "Dollar Bill is autistic. Autism means he thinks differently than we do, but with early intervention there would be a great improvement. He has to be evaluated and he has to go to a special school so that they might train him to think more like we think."

Dollar Bill started to go to the special school so that his social skills would develop. He also would be evaluated at the special school and be placed in the proper setting for improvement.

Dollar Bill began to play with his brothers, 2-Bits, 4-Bits, and 6 Bits were so happy that Dollar Bill was getting better with his social skills.

Mama Beez was happy that Dollar Bill was now playing with his brothers and having fun. She was happy; too, that 2-Bits, 4-Bits, and 6-Bits seem to understand and had learned a lot about autism.

The therapist had told her that the entire family had to understand their autistic brother because his disability was the whole family's disability.

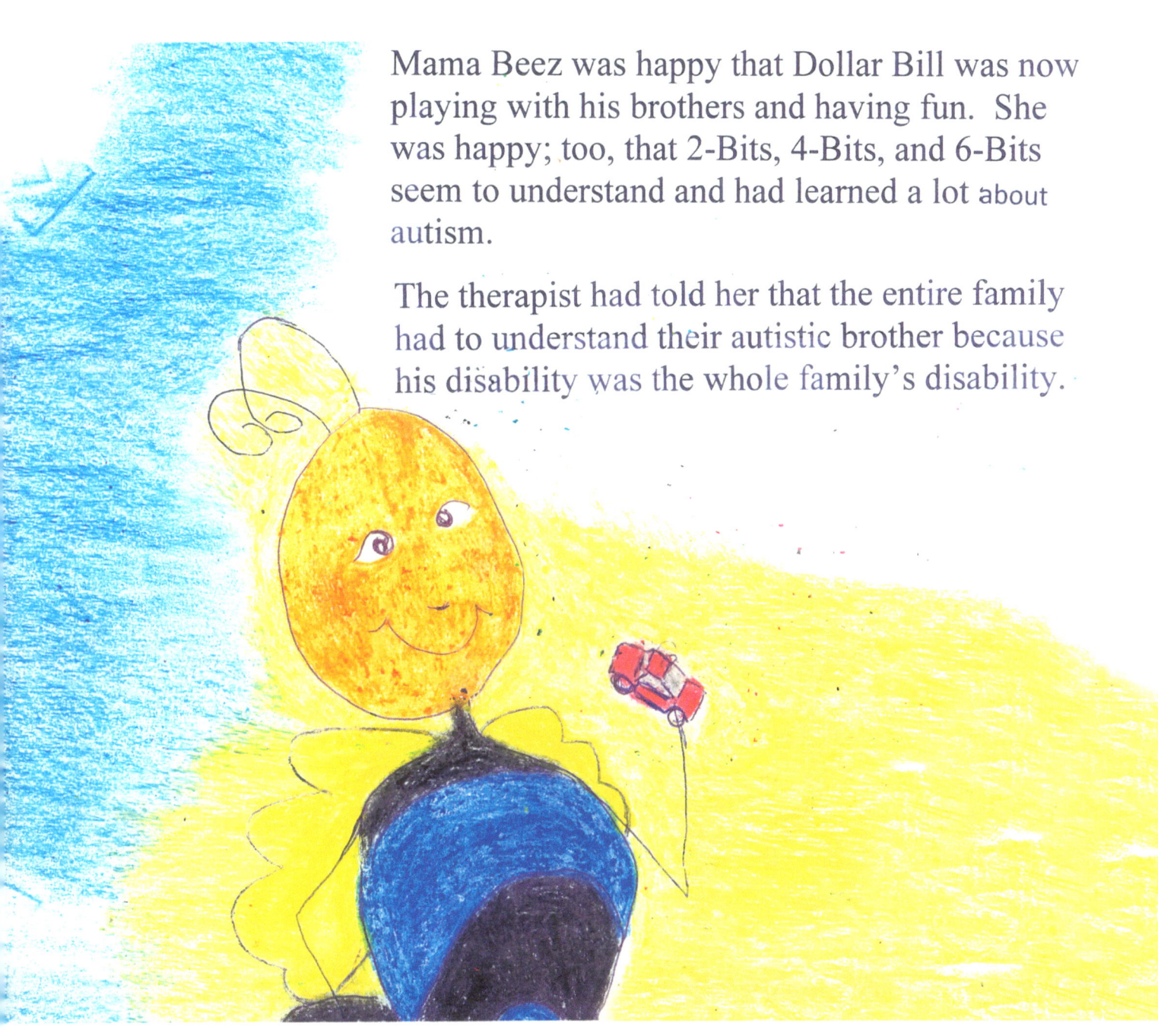

Dollar Bill went to a special school and had fun going.

His favorite—riding the big, yellow school bus. He looked forward to riding on the school bus each day. The bus picked him up and brought him back home. Dollar bill would happily wave good-bye, stand and watch until the bus was no longer in sight.

www.ingramcontent.com/pod-product-compliance
Lightning Source LLC
LaVergne TN
LVHW070452080526
838202LV00035B/2805